KB267591

해리엇 지퍼트 글

해리엇 지퍼트는 미국에서 태어나 자랐습니다. 초등학교 교사와 교육과정 개발자를 거쳐
어린이 독자를 위한 책을 쓰는 작가가 되었답니다. 저서로는 《안나의 빨간 외투》,
《졸린 개》, 《무슨 색이 될까?》 등이 있습니다.

에밀리 볼람 그림

에밀리 볼람은 영국 브라이턴 대학에서 미술을 공부한 뒤 그림책 일러스트레이터로
활동하며 많은 그림을 그렸습니다. 주요 작품으로 《무슨 색이 될까?》, 《많이! 많이!》,
《행복한 집》 등이 있습니다.

꼬마 당나귀 버찌 ❻

BUZZY'S BIG BEDTIME BOOK

1판 1쇄 2013년 12월 20일

지은이 해리엇 지퍼트 **그린이** 에밀리 볼람
펴낸이 정연금 **펴낸곳** 멘토르
책임편집 이수정 **기획** 김미숙, 강지예, 조원선, 안소영
마케팅 나길훈 **경영지원** 안정배, 박은정
등록 2004년 12월 30일 제302-2004-00081호
주소 서울시 마포구 동교동 198-5번지 신흥빌딩 3층
전화 02-706-0911 **팩스** 02-706-0913 **홈페이지** www.mentorbook.co.kr
ISBN 978-89-6305-663-0 (14840)

BUZZY'S BIG BEDTIME BOOK

Harriet Ziefert · Emily Bolam

PART 1

Bathtime

Night is coming,
bedtime's near.

Daddy says, "Buzzy, bathtime, dear."

The tub is filled,
the water's fine.

Daddy says, "Buzzy, wash-up time."

"Doesn't it feel good
once you're in?"

Daddy says, "Buzzy,
lift your chin."

Bath is ending, so is play.

Daddy says,
"Buzzy, put your boats away."

Water's swirling—
glug... glug... glug!

Daddy says,

"Buzzy, give me the plug."

Buzzy's worried.
What's he to do?

Could the drain
suck him down too?

Daddy says, "Buzzy,
no need to frown."

"That **drain** could never suck you down!"

Good night!

Good night.
Sleep tight.

Not ready?

Why?

I want to hear
another story.

No more stories.
Good night.

Sleep tight.
I am turning off the light.

But I want
a drink.
No drink.
Good night.

Sleep tight.
I am turning off the light.

Where's Teddy?
I need him.

Teddy bear... all right.
Here he is.

Now good night.
Sleep tight.
I am turning off the light.

A hug and kiss...
all right.

Now good night.
Sleep tight.
I am turning off the light.

It's dark in here.
I see a shadow
—and it's moving!
MOMMY! MOMMY!

What's wrong,
dear?

I'm scared, Mommy.
I need a night-light.

Night-light... all right.

Sleep tight.
Now good night!

I'm NOT scared.
I'm all right.
I'll sleep tight.

Good night,
Buzzy!

세이펜과 함께 읽는
꼬마 당나귀 버찌 시리즈

표지의 나레이션 아이콘과 액팅 아이콘을 누르면
각각의 스타일로 전체 듣기를 할 수 있어요.

세이펜으로 그림을 찍으면 배경음과
함께 2쪽 단위로 책을 읽어 줍니다.

세이펜으로 글자를 누르면
해당 문장을 들을 수 있어요.

꼬마 당나귀 버찌 시리즈는 한글 동화 6권, 영어 동화 6권,
총 12권으로 구성된 한영 쌍둥이책이에요.

꼬마 당나귀 버찌 시리즈 한글 동화(전 6권)

꼬마 당나귀 버찌 시리즈 영어 동화(전 6권)

영문판 구입 문의: 070-7568-2653

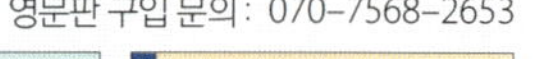

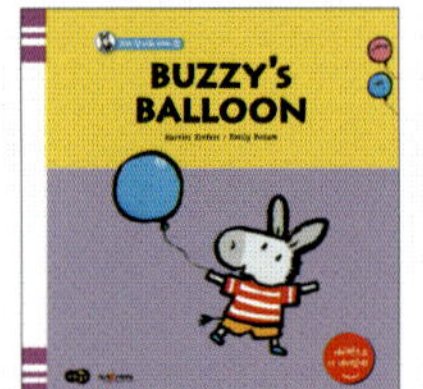

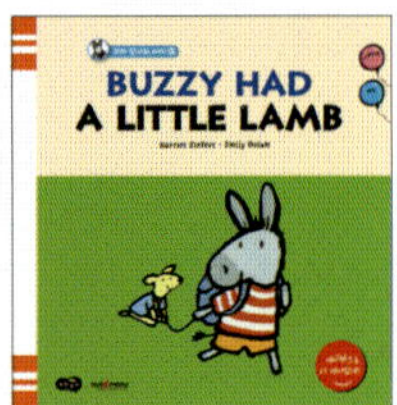

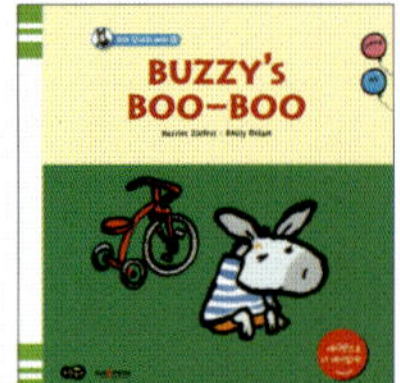

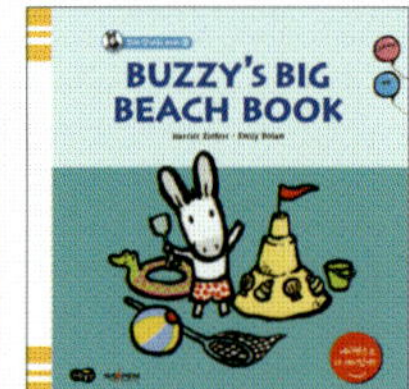

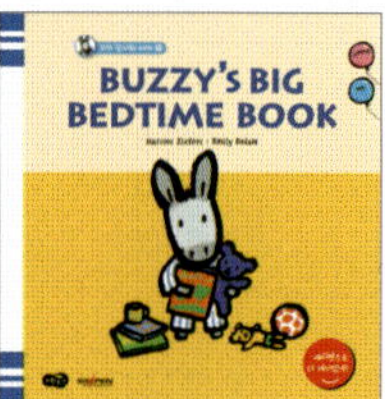

네이버 카페 심봉사09에 방문하면 노란우산 도서에 대한 정보와 다국어 관련 스터디를 보실 수 있습니다. http://cafe.naver.com/simbongsa09